Jill Paton Walsh

MATTHEW
Sea Singer *and the*

Illustrated by Alan Marks

SIMON & SCHUSTER
YOUNG BOOKS

JF

For Alex and Vicky

$$\frac{7140}{5}$$

First published in Great Britain in 1992
by Simon & Schuster Young Books
Campus 400
Maylands Avenue
Hemel Hempstead
Herts HP2 7EZ

Typeset in 15pt Garamond Light by
Goodfellow & Egan Ltd., Cambridge
Printed and bound in Portugal by Edicoes ASA

British Library Cataloguing in Publication Data available

ISBN 0 7500 1175 0
ISBN 0 7500 1176 9 (pbk)

Chapter One

Once there was a little girl called Birdy who paid a shilling for a living boy. Birdy's father, Papajack, was a ferryman, rowing travellers across the river.

Now one morning Papajack rowed a man
across the river, who had with him a raggedy
little boy. He was an orphan master, it
seemed, and he had taken Matthew – for that
was the raggedy boy's name – to a farmer
who wanted a boy, and would pay a shilling
to have one. But when they got there the
farmer wouldn't have the boy because he
didn't look strong enough for the work.
"Stunted" the farmer had called him.

"He might grow if you fed him," said Birdy.

"Food costs money," said the orphan master. "And it's all his fault, for not eating up his gruel like he should."

"I don't know whose fault it is," said Papajack, "but I know a hungry child when I see one."

And Birdy took her birthday shilling out of her apron pocket, and bought Matthew, on the spot.

Chapter Two

Next morning, Birdy woke up hearing
something new. There was the wind scraping
itself on the sharp corners of the house and
whining a bit over it, as it often and often did.
And there was the sea, sighing and shushing
itself, as it often and often did; but winding in
among those familiar noises was another, a
new one, flowing.

Birdy got up and looked down from the sleeping loft, and sure enough it was raggedy Matthew, sitting on his blanket by the embers of the hearth, and singing to himself, very softly. He was singing as a bird sings, a song sound without words, a song shape without tunes, and the sound wove in and out of the wind and waves, like a streamlet of water falling in a steep little valley.

Birdy sat still as a mouse, and listened, and soon her mother and father were awake and listening too.

"I don't know what to make of that," said Papajack over breakfast. "It has a faery feel to it. I think we'll take him over to the parson at Zennor, by and by, and see what he says about it."

So that very afternoon, while Papajack
minded the ferry, Birdy and her mother took
raggedy Matthew, and went up over and
along to Zennor, and got him to sing to the
parson.

Well, the parson didn't call it faery singing.
He called it an untaught voice of great natural
beauty, and he wanted to keep Matthew in
his house, and teach him words to go along
with the notes, and have him in the choir on
Sundays. He offered Birdy the shilling for
him.

"No," said Birdy. "I know better than to go buying and selling a child, even if the orphan master didn't. I don't hold with it."

"You are dead right," said the parson. "Or living right. But I'm sorry you should lose a shilling. I would give it gladly."

"Keep your shilling, and give Matthew a day in the week to play with me," said Birdy, and so it was agreed.

Chapter Three

Time went by and by and Matthew learned
tunes with his notes, and words with his
tunes. He learned to sing the Sunday music
in Zennor church. He had a voice that might
have been an angel's voice. Whatever folk
hoped for in heaven, Matthew's singing made
them think of it. He made mothers think of
the children sleeping safe and warm; he
made the children think of dancing barefoot,

or of flying under the stars; he made the
fishermen think of the hold full of fishes; he
made the farmers think of the harvest safely
in; and the shepherds think of lambs all
gathered in the fold. You never heard people
singing the chorus and amen to a hymn the
way folk sang back to Matthew in the little
church at Zennor on Sundays.

And people began saying that on Sundays when the service started at Zennor, the birds on the bush fell silent, and the wheeling gulls stopped screaming, and the seal-folk and mermaids gathered on the rocks below the church, hoping to catch, drifting down to them on the wind, the faint sound of Matthew singing.

Chapter Four

Then one day Matthew went missing. All day
Birdy thought the parson had kept Matthew,
and the parson thought he was with Birdy.
They didn't find out they were wrong till
Matthew had been gone many hours. The
parson fetched out all the boys in the choir to
go running from door to door, knocking and
calling; the men went searching the cliff foot,
and the women the cliff top; and when
darkness fell you could see lanterns
wandering everywhere like fireflies, high
and low, but there wasn't a sign of Matthew.

All night he didn't come home, nor all next day. By the next night the harbour master put an end to searching. "The waves will give him back to us, in a day or two, most likely," he said, and he meant they would find the boy drowned. The parson's eyes were red from crying, for he loved his singing boy dearly; and Birdy sat as cold and quiet as a stone, fretting herself about Matthew.

Right up to the following Sunday there wasn't sight nor sound of Matthew. In church the parson prayed "Lord let us hear of him, living or dead . . ." The choir boys did their best, but they sounded all hoarse and leaden, and Birdy ran out of the church door before the service was over, because it upset her so much. She went down the steep little path to the sea. She hadn't got half way down before she could see the three-stone skerries, the seal rocks standing off shore. And there wasn't a seal to be seen there!

There wasn't a seal, nor a mermaid, nor so
much as a cormorant stood there. And hadn't
they been lurking every Sunday to catch the
sound of the choir? Hadn't they been
lumbering out of the water, and waiting for
the wind to bring voices down to them?
Specially one voice?

Suddenly Birdy knew where Matthew was.

Chapter Five

Getting him back, though, was another
matter. Birdy knew how to make the seal-
queen come and talk to her. She stood on the
beach, and she talked about seal hunters,
about endless trouble and grief. She talked
about iron and axes, and no rock being safe
for a seal pup.

By and by the seal-queen popped her head out of the waves, and climbed on to a rock for a parley. She was a strange sort of sea creature, a half-in-half kind of thing, mostly like a seal, though some would have called her a selkie, and some would have called her a mermaid.

"Stealing's nasty," Birdy told her.
"Stealing's *mustn't!* And stealing a person is
worst of all wicked things. Give him back."

"Shan't!" said the seal-queen. "He isn't
yours by blood or family. He isn't anyone's.
We'd never take a blood brother or sister or
child," she added smugly. "We know better'n
that. But Matthew ain't yours at all, so potter
off, Birdy!"

"He is so!" Birdy said. "He's mine because I bought him; and taking him is stealing and I want him back!"

"What did you pay for him?" the seal-queen asked. "I'll buy him from you!"

"Just an ordinary shilling," said Birdy.

Well, you should have seen what the sea-people brought to her! Great piles of pearls; handfuls of fine gold coins out of shipwrecks; bits of jewels; Spanish doubloons; a great long necklace of moonstones in shining silver, till the sand at her feet looked like a king's treasure except for the strands of seaweed tangled up in it.

Birdy stood there stony-faced, and she
didn't touch a thing of it, nor even look at it
properly. But when at last the sea-people
stopped bringing things, and stayed quiet,
circled round her, she said:

"You haven't got a shilling, have you?"

"There's the worth of a million shillings
there, girl!" said the seal-queen.

"Just one shilling is the price," said Birdy. "And I want it exact, or I want Matthew back. Or else the sea-people are thieves, and we'll hunt you to death!"

"Give us time, and we'll find one. We'll sift the sands of England grain by grain. There's sure to be a dropped one somewhere . . ."

"No," said Birdy. "Give him back now." And was she glad that she'd refused the parson's shilling!

"Shan't!" said the seal-queen. "Oh Birdy, it ain't fair, it ain't fair! There's all the land children singing so sweetly, and there isn't a one of ours but sounds like old rocks rubbed together! I've just got to have Matthew for keeps! I can't bear to be without the sound of him, and that's the truth, and if you hunt us because of it, well, you'll just have to hunt us, that's all!"

Birdy sat down on the sand then, with all the treasure shining round her, to think. And by and by she said to the seal-queen, "Lookee here. If the parson was to teach one of your pups to sing really sweetly, would you give Matthew back then?"

"He couldn't," said the seal-queen. "You want to hear them!"

"He might be able to," said Birdy.

"He wouldn't," said the seal-queen. "Those parsons-on-the land have a down on us poor sea heathens, in the water."

"I'll ask him," said Birdy, and she got up, and plodded back up the cliff path, to find the grieving parson and tell him where Matthew was, and what they'd have to do to get him back.

Chapter Six

It wasn't easy. The seal-child was dreadfully
unhappy on land, and at first it wouldn't sing
at all. It didn't speak even as much English as
the seal-queen. Only Birdy could understand
it, and she did it by guessing. It was
dreadfully unwieldy too, for it couldn't walk,
having no legs. Below the waist it was just a
great thick scaly tail, with a frill of fins at the
girdle. Above the waist it looked roughly like
a human child, though its skin was a greeny
sort of colour, with a mackerel sheen on it,
and its hair was like the bright green seaweed that floats in the summer shallows.

Birdy looked after it as best she could. She couldn't carry it more than a few steps – it was nearly as big as she was – so she borrowed a wheelbarrow to trundle it in. By and by she guessed one thing that was wrong with it was being dry, so she put it to sleep in Mamalucy's washtub, brim full of seawater. It curled up and went to sleep right under the water, with only its seaweed hair floating on top.

31

And what could she give it to eat? It didn't seem right to offer it grilled mackerel, or starry-gazy pie, Birdy's favourite, with the fishes' heads poked through the pie-crust. Luckily it took to porridge sweetened with wild honey.

Hardest of all was to hit on a name for it;
neither a fish nor a fellow as it was and, come
to that, either a fellow or a lass, there was no
telling which.

"One thing's sure, it was never christened
anything," said Papajack, and so Birdy called
it "Pagan" and that seemed to fit.

It was a quandary how to keep Pagan wet
in singing lessons. There was an answer to
that, of course, but it caused a scandal. A
sea-green heathen splashing about in the
font and trying to hit a high note! And for a
long while Pagan couldn't seem to catch on
to the idea of singing. He barked, like dogs
or seals. The parson played him notes on the
organ, and he mewed and screamed like a
gull. He could shush and hiss like a wave-

breaking, and gurgle like the sea sucking at
the rock pools. He could rattle like pebbles,
and whine and howl like the storm winds,
but he couldn't seem to sing a note! He was
such a horrible scholar that it broke the
parson's heart to have to teach him, but he
didn't give up – he went on playing notes to
Pagan, and coaxing him and urging him, and
playing again, till you'd have thought that the
font itself would have got the hang of it.

Then one day Birdy was wheeling Pagan home again, when she stopped for a rest. The two of them sat for a while on the beach, Birdy on a rock, and Pagan in his wheelbarrow, watching the waves. And suddenly they could hear Matthew singing! Just as faint and far away as he had once sounded to the fishermen sailing by Zennor, or the seal-people basking on the skerries below the headland, so he sounded now to Birdy, singing under the calm waters, somewhere far out and deep under. So faint and far away you could only just catch the sound if you stayed very still and quiet. But it was Matthew all right; no mistaking his golden voice.

Birdy said to Pagan, "If only you sounded like that, Pagan, we'd have you home again in no time, swimming in the chilly water, and Matthew sitting close by the fire, eating starry-gazy pie!"

And Pagan stared at her with his great big rock-pool eyes, and she saw a glint in them that looked like someone catching on.

Chapter Seven

The next day he began singing as soon as they put him in the font, and strange sort of singing it was, too. You couldn't hardly hear him he was so faint; as faint as though miles of distance had spun the sound out thin, and hearing him cast a shadow in your mind. But there wasn't any doubt it was singing, and beautiful in its way. Only they couldn't make him sing up.

"He's only heard Matthew from far away!" declared Birdy. "That's what it is!"

So the parson sent her running round the parish to find the choir boys, fetching them from the farmyards and the sheep-runs, and the sail-lofts, and the fish-market, and they came in their working clothes, and folk flocked along with them, and they all stood round the font and raised their voices, and sang to Pagan loud enough to raise the roof on Zennor Church:

"*Praise him from whom all blessings flow!*
Praise him all creatures here below! . . ."

And then at last the mer-child opened his mouth, and *really* sang! And it was terrible music he sang. Whatever you were afraid of in the world, that song made you think of it. He made fishermen think of drowning, he made women think of hungry children, and larders bare, and farmers of rainstorms at haytime, and children of parents vanished,

and parents of lost children, and the parson of losing his hearing, and Birdy of losing her sight. His song sounded of shipwreck and loss and ruin . . . but you couldn't deny it was beautiful. It was as beautiful as great tempests on stormy waters, or the love of the living for the dead.

"Good enough," said the parson, though he was looking ash-white. So the ringers rolled up their sleeves, and they rang the bells. The sound of bells on a mid-week morning brought the people from far and near and all over Zennor parish crowding down to the shore, and the seal-people flocking to the rocks.

Birdy brought Pagan to the dry side of the water's edge, and the seal-queen brought Matthew to the nearest rock inshore.

"Let's be hearing him, then," she said. "I'll hear them both together, to compare them fairly."

Then Pagan set up his dark singing, and in a few bars Matthew raised his voice and joined in. And while they were singing together, you could grasp the whole world in your mind. You could think of hunger and plenty, of storms and calm, of exile and homecoming, of death and birth, all together, the whole creation dark side up, and bright side up like night and day in the same moment . . .

Folk could have listened for a hundred years, but in a few moments the seal-queen said, "Not a pebble to choose between them! Have him back then!" And the wonderful singing was stopped, and Pagan leapt and slithered to the water's edge, and swimming as graceful as a bird flies he was gone, and Matthew was wading ashore.

So that was that for then. But folk say that when the ferryman's daughter at Lelant grew up and got married, she didn't get a wedding gift from the bridegroom, only an old shilling with barnacles on it. And they say her young man had a fine deep voice like a church bell; and they say if he sang by the edge of the sea, you would hear someone singing in answer, in a high faint treble, as icy and bright and distant as the stars in a winter sky. You could think of the whole world at once, hearing that.